John Michael Callison

May God Bless
you as you
read this story

Faith, Hope
and the
Giant

John Callison

ISBN 978-1-64670-699-0 (Paperback)
ISBN 978-1-64670-700-3 (Hardcover)
ISBN 978-1-64670-701-0 (Digital)

Registration number for the copyright of Faith, Hope and the
Giant TXu 2-156-140 effective May 29, 2019

Covenant Books, Inc.
11661 Hwy 707
Murrells Inlet, SC 29576
www.covenantbooks.com

The story, Faith, Hope and the Giant, is dedicated to my ninety-three year old mother, Jo Callison. Mom's life has been a true example of the description of love in the New Testament. Love is patient, love is kind, love is not arrogant, love is not easily angered, love always hopes, trusts, and rejoices in truth. Mom's faith, wisdom, and humor has touched the lives of countless people. From West Virginia to Colorado and now in Texas, she has demonstrated to many people what the love of God is truly like. I can't imagine anyone having a greater gift in their life than in having a wonderful, Godly mother.

The Story of "Faith Hope and The Giant" is illustrated by Lidia Ostapiuk Earl.

Lidia was born in Ternopil, Ukraine.in 1941. Her family fled the Ukraine when Lidia was a young child, to escape the takeover of their country by the Russian communists. Lidia and her family lived in displaced persons camps in Germany when she was growing up. She remembers playing among the rubble of old bombs and artillery as a small child. It was in these camps that she received "care Packages" from a wonderful country called America. The "care packages" included watercolor sets which her grandfather, a teacher and religious artist, used to paint beautiful Bible pictures for Lidia. After coming to America in 1950 Lidia continued with the artwork her grandfather inspired. She has studied, taught and practiced drawing and painting her entire life. You now see a part of her work in the pictures featured in "Faith, Hope and the Giant"

Faith, Hope and the Giant

Long ago, in a land far away, there was a beautiful valley that people called Rich Valley. It was easy to see why people gave the valley its name. The valley was full of wonderful things that should have made living in Rich Valley a very pleasant experience. The valley had all kinds of beautiful trees. There were trees that produced apples, pears, oranges, figs, cherries, plums, and persimmons. There were also trees that yielded nuts like pecans, walnuts, chestnuts, and hazelnuts. The land in the valley was rich and deep. You could grow almost anything in Rich Valley. The people grew wheat, barley, oats, potatoes, tomatoes, corn, beets, and almost anything else they could think of. In the middle of the valley ran a beautiful river, which the people named Crystal River. The water was clear and deep. You could see all types of fish swimming, as the sun reflected off the dazzling pebbles that lined the river bottom. The children in Rich Valley loved to swim and fish in the river, but they were not the only ones that enjoyed the river. Animals like deer, fox, bear, raccoons, rabbits, and otters also loved coming to the river. Then there were the tall pine trees that stretched to the sky in Rich Valley. The people used the tall pines to build amazing log cabins. The cabins had large, stone fireplaces inside, which kept people warm on the coldest winter day. The cabins were kept cool in the summer by the chilled mountain breezes, which prevented Rich Valley from ever getting too hot.

Rich Valley should have been about the best place in the world to live, but there was a problem. The people in Rich Valley were frightened. If it was a cold day in Rich Valley, the people were certain that the cold would last forever, and springtime would never return. If it was a hot day in Rich Valley, the people were sure the sun had moved closer to the earth, and they would all melt in the heat. If someone in Rich Valley was a little bit sick, the people were certain a terrible illness would wipe out the entire population of Rich Valley. Everyone in Rich Valley was scared of one thing or another. Strangers who visited Rich Valley were puzzled by all this. They asked the people why they were so afraid when they lived in such a beautiful valley with all kinds of food and natural treasures.

The oldest man in Rich Valley said he had the answer. "Long ago," said the old man, "an *Evil Wizard* came to Rich Valley on his way home to Ice Mountain. He hated the people of Rich Valley, because they were all so happy. He saw the people laughing and playing and enjoying all the wonderful natural treasures that Rich Valley had. The Evil Wizard could not stand to see people having such pleasure in life. He lived a cold and bitter life on Ice Mountain, with no one but his *evil servant* to share his misery. So, the Wizard decided to cast an evil spell upon the people of Rich Valley."

As the Evil Wizard was leaving the valley he had just visited, he turned and proclaimed his evil curse upon the people:

PEOPLE OF RICH VALLEY, MY WORDS YOU SHALL HEAR
THE WORDS I WILL SPEAK, WHICH WILL CAUSE YOU TO FEAR
JOY INTO SORROW, AND LAUGHTER TO TEARS
YOU WILL ALWAYS BE AFRAID FOR ALL OF YOUR YEARS

"Then the Wizard carved the curse on the giant pine tree at the entrance to Rich Valley so everyone could read it, in case they had not heard him," said the old man.

"I remember he laughed as he left the valley, because he had destroyed any chance of happiness for the people of Rich Valley," declared the old man's wife. "That is why all the people in Rich Valley live in fear," she explained to the visitors to Rich Valley. "No one knows how to break the curse, and so it is our destiny to always live in fear."

So, the people in Rich Valley lived in fear for many years. It seemed that living in fear was something they could not escape, as if the hidden power of the Wizard's curse would always control their lives. A darkness settled over Rich Valley, and it seemed that the Evil

Wizard had won. Some people wanted to destroy the Wizard's curse, but they did not know how. All the people in Rich Valley wished they could return to the days when they laughed and loved and enjoyed the beauty surrounding them, but the curse remained. No one, young or old, in Rich Valley was quite sure how the evil curse of fear could ever be broken.

The Giant

It was in the spring of the year when someone arrived in Rich Valley that caused the people to be even more afraid than they usually were. No one had ever seen anyone like the *Giant*. He was at least two feet taller than the tallest man in Rich Valley. His arms, shoulders, legs, and hands were twice the size of any man the people had ever seen. He seemed so powerful as he walked through the valley that he could have crushed stones with his bare hands, if he had wanted to. He was first spotted walking into the valley on Glory Road, which went from Snow Mountain into the center of town. This was where most of the people had built their log cabins, along the Crystal River.

When the people saw him, they ran inside their houses and bolted their doors. Mothers hugged their frightened children and told them not to cry out, for fear the Giant might hear them and investigate. No one even thought of approaching the Giant or talking to him. He looked much too powerful to dare come near him. Everyone hid in their homes, or in the deep woods, and hoped he would simply go away. As the Giant walked through town, he looked at all the things around him. The beautiful trees in the valley had their first fruits just starting to grow. The crops in the field were green and almost ready for harvest. The Giant saw the splendid Crystal River and all the fish swimming in its clear waters. *What a beautiful place*, thought the Giant, and yet, even as he enjoyed the beauty, a tear slowly came down his cheek. He realized that all the people in this delightful valley were afraid of him. It was a feeling he was all too familiar with. As he came to the end of the valley, he saw the giant pine tree where the Evil Wizard had engraved his curse long ago:

PEOPLE OF RICH VALLEY, MY WORDS YOU SHALL HEAR
THE WORDS I WILL SPEAK, WHICH WILL CAUSE YOU TO FEAR
JOY INTO SORROW, AND LAUGHTER TO TEARS
YOU WILL ALWAYS BE AFRAID, FOR ALL OF YOUR YEARS

No wonder everyone is afraid of me, thought the Giant. *A curse of fear has been put upon these people.* The Giant shook his head sadly. He was losing hope that he would ever find a place where people would love and accept him as he had wished for so long.

Just then, the Giant saw a man step out from behind a giant pine tree. The man was different than any man the Giant had ever seen. His face was shining, and his clothes looked like they had been made of tiny stars. The Giant was startled and even a little afraid.

"Who are you?" said the Giant to the stranger.

"Don't be afraid," said the stranger smiling. "I am here to help you if I can."

The Giant was puzzled. *Why would this stranger help me?* he thought. *I have never seen him before, and yet he seems to have a kindness toward me.*

"Do you know me?" asked the Giant.

"You are the adopted son of Jacob, the stone mason from Dark River Valley," said the stranger. "I saw you when Jacob first took you in as a small child. Your family had all died of the fever that swept through Dark River Valley. Jacob's wife and young son also died of the fever, and someone brought you to him."

Now the Giant wept openly. This man seemed to know all about him. "How is my father?" asked the Giant as he wiped the tears away.

"Jacob is well," answered the stranger, "though he misses you greatly."

The Giant's mind went quickly back in time. He could not remember his real family. He had been too young when they had all died of the terrible fever. He thought back to the kind man who had raised him. Jacob had taught him so many things. He had taught him how to work with rock. He had shown him how to cut and shape the rock to build walls and houses. He had taught him the use of clay and mortar, to hold the rock together. But Jacob had taught him other things, things that mattered more than rock and mortar. He had taught him about love and having compassion for other people. Even when the other children made fun of him for his great size, Jacob had gently encouraged him to forgive them.

"Joshua," his father would say, "do not let their teasing change your good nature. Someday many people will recognize your loving, gentle spirit, and they will be drawn to it."

The Giant smiled at the memory of his adopted father. Only a few people had ever called him by his real name. To most people, he was only "the Giant." At ten years of age, he had already grown to the size of a large, powerful man. Most of the other children had been afraid to play with him because of his size and strength. Joshua had been treated like a stranger by most of the people in Dark River Valley. He was too different for them to accept him or befriend him in some manner.

"Father," he once told Jacob, "I feel like someone on the outside, always looking in at all the others."

Jacob had felt his son's sadness. He knew only a few kind people had ever taken time to discover what a loving, compassionate boy Joshua really was.

"Perhaps someday you will find a place where people will take time to know who you really are," Jacob had told Joshua many times.

Joshua had been so lost in his thoughts; he had forgotten all about the stranger. He looked up and talked to him once again.

"Do you really know my father, Jacob?" he asked the bright stranger.

"I have known your father for many years," the shiny man replied. "I will tell him I have seen you in Rich Valley. He will be pleased you have found such a beautiful place to live."

Joshua thought for moment. Rich Valley was a beautiful place. In fact, he had never seen any place with so much life and natural wonder. Yet Joshua sensed there was also a cold darkness about Rich Valley. He had felt it, as he had walked through the valley when he first arrived. The places children should have been playing and where people would normally be gathered were empty. There was a sadness in the air he could feel but not explain.

"I must tell you, kind stranger," Joshua said, "I am not sure the people here will ever accept me. They seem to have a curse of fear upon them."

The shining man looked at Joshua with a great sense of compassion.

"I know you are discouraged, Joshua. I have seen the curse left by the Evil Wizard, and I too have felt the shadow that has been cast upon this valley," said the stranger.

Joshua felt a sense of relief. At least there was someone who understood him. He did not feel quite as alone as he had felt before. Joshua and his newfound friend talked a little while longer until a sudden gust of cold mountain wind stung Joshua's eyes. He rubbed them for a few moments, but when he looked up, his newfound friend was gone. Joshua ran to the place where the shiny man had been standing. He looked in every direction, but there was no one to be seen. He stood for a moment in the shadow of the tall pine tree. Had he been dreaming? Had he imagined the shining stranger? It had all seemed so real. It had been so wonderful to talk to someone who knew about him. *It could not have been a dream*, he thought. How would a stranger have known about his father? How would a stranger have known so much about his life? As Joshua looked down, he saw fresh footprints in the black soil beside the pine tree. It had not been a dream after all. Suddenly he was hopeful once again. He had felt the warmth and kindness in the shining man's voice. Now he remembered the last thing his newfound friend had told him.

"Remember, dear friend," the bright man had said, "in the moment when all hope seems lost, somewhere a light is shining."

Joshua looked once more where the shiny man had been standing.

"Perhaps someday I can help remove the curse of fear from this valley," he said to himself.

A New Family

Summertime in Rich Valley saw a new family arrive from a faraway place called Promise Mountain. The new family had traveled for many weeks to come to Rich Valley because they had heard of all the natural wonders and beauty of the valley. When they arrived, some of the people warned them about the curse of fear that had been put on the valley by the Evil Wizard. The oldest man in town took the father of the family, Joseph, and showed him the curse written on the tall pine tree.

> PEOPLE OF RICH VALLEY, MY WORDS YOU SHALL HEAR
> THE WORDS I WILL SPEAK, WHICH WILL CAUSE YOU TO FEAR
> JOY INTO SORROW, AND LAUGHTER TO TEARS
> YOU WILL ALWAYS BE AFRAID FOR ALL OF YOUR YEARS

A number of people from the valley had followed Joseph and the old man to see if the curse the Wizard had carved there still remained. It appeared unchanged, as if it had been engraved there only yesterday. The people wondered if the new family would flee when they realized the power of the Wizard's curse of fear. Joseph looked at the curse carefully for a long time. He turned to the crowd of people that had gathered by the old pine tree.

"You know," he said thoughtfully, "I am a carpenter by trade. Perhaps someday I can take my carpenter tools and remove the awful curse from this tree."

Many of the people gasped at the idea of removing the curse. They were so frightened by the Wizard's power that they trembled to even think about touching it. Here was a man unafraid, who spoke of removing it. The people thought perhaps he did not fully realize just how powerful the Evil Wizard really was. Nevertheless, the idea that someone even thought of abolishing the curse gave the people a hint of hopefulness they had not had in many years.

As Joseph returned to Rich Valley, with the crowd of people, a young girl ran to greet him. She had golden hair with curls and blue eyes that seemed to dance in the sunlight.

When the people asked about her, Joseph said, "This is my oldest daughter, Faith. Perhaps I can tell you a story about her so you will understand who she is. When Faith was a child, her mother, Grace, taught her about healing. They walked all over the hills and valleys around Promise Mountain looking for herbs and roots and berries that helped people get well when they were sick. Faith loved learning about everything in life. Grace taught her to read when she was only four, and she read every book she could find in the villages around Promise Mountain. When Faith was ten, she and her mother were looking for healing herbs on Promise Mountain. As they were looking, Faith found a man named Simon who was badly wounded from a fall off the mountain. Simon was a sheep herder who lived alone on Promise Mountain because he did not trust people. Simon had told everyone that people had only hurt and betrayed him, and so he lived a solitary, friendless life. Faith and Grace helped him to his little cottage, then bandaged and doctored his wounds. For two weeks, they took care of him until he finally was able to walk again.

"One day, Faith smiled at Simon and said, 'Simon, you must get better. Your sheep are missing you.'

"For the first time in his life, Simon laughed. In all his life, he had never felt that anyone had truly cared about him or loved him. After Grace and Faith saved him, he was never the same again. The people of Promise Mountain marveled at how friendly and caring Simon became. It was hard to believe the generous, friendly man had once been a lonely hermit."

As Joseph finished his story, his wife, Grace, arrived. She was a lovely woman, and the people immediately perceived her as a thoughtful, compassionate person.

Joseph turned to her and asked, "What was it that caused Simon to change and become so welcoming?"

"I think," said Grace with a smile, "a little touch of Faith was all Simon ever needed."

Just then another young girl with dark hair and eyes like green emeralds ran and jumped into Joseph's arms. He tossed her high in the air as she shrieked with laughter.

"This is my youngest daughter, Hope," said Joseph. "She is the singer and musician in our family."

"Can you sing the people a song, Hope?" asked Grace lovingly.

Hope began singing a song about a little red hen who had lost her chicks and searched high and low to find them. When she finished, the people all clapped their hands and laughed. It had been a long time since there was singing and laughter in Rich Valley.

The sun began to go down, and Joseph and Grace gathered their two daughters to get ready to sleep in the wagon that had brought them to Rich Valley. Faith and Hope waved good-bye to the crowd as they walked with their parents to their camp beside the Crystal River. As the crowd of people walked back to their homes, they talked about the new family.

"There is something about that family that gives me courage," said one woman to her husband.

"Yes," he answered, "I had a sense of peace when the little girl sang her song. I have not felt that way in many years."

As Joseph, Grace, Faith, and Hope disappeared in the distance, an older woman in the crowd remembered the days when there was wonder and song and cheerfulness in the valley. A tear ran down her cheek, and she wished, as the tear fell to the ground, that somehow joy would return to the people in Rich Valley. She was not alone in that wish.

The Meeting

Joshua had been busy since his meeting with the shiny man at the old pine tree. He had decided not to enter Rich Valley for a while since the people were so frightened of him. He also knew that as long as the Evil Wizard's curse of fear was present in the valley, no one would dare approach or talk to him. Still, Joshua had a sense of hope, and so he decided to build a house on the rocky hills near Rich Valley. For weeks, he cut and shaped stones to build his house, as his father Jacob had taught him. It wasn't long before he had enough stones cut and shaped to build a huge house. However, there was nothing to do but work, and soon a feeling of loneliness began to overtake him. Knowing the people of Rich Valley were too scared to talk to him, Joshua began developing a friendship with all the animals that lived around him. Soon the deer, squirrels, rabbits, and birds were eating out of his huge hands. The animals sensed the gentleness of the giant man and were unafraid of him. Joshua took pleasure in his newfound friends. He wished for the companionship of humans, but the animals gave him a sense of sharing and belonging that he needed. Every day Joshua cut and shaped new stones for his house and then spent time feeding and playing with the animals.

One day, after he finished working, he walked through the woods to gather nuts and berries for his animals. As he was walking, he thought he heard someone in the distance singing. He stopped and listened closely. Perhaps it was a bird or maybe the wind rustling through the trees. No, it was the voice of a child singing. *I hope I am not going crazy*, he thought. He continued walking toward the sound when suddenly he saw a flash of golden hair in a distant clearing. Joshua didn't know what to think or do. *If it is some children, they will scream and run away like all the others*, he thought. Still, he longed for the sound of a human voice, and so he continued toward the clearing. When he came to the edge of the clearing, he saw something that made him laugh out loud. Two little girls seemed to be gathering berries and putting them into baskets, as if it were a game. The first little girl had golden hair and blue eyes that sparkled in the sunlight. The second little girl had dark hair and eyes like green emeralds. The girls looked up when Joshua laughed, but they did not run. Instead they walked toward him, as if they knew him. Joshua was stunned. No stranger had ever approached him with such confidence.

The girl with the golden hair looked at Joshua from head to toe before she spoke.

"You are the tallest person I have ever seen. Are you a giant?" she asked.

Joshua didn't know what to say. There was a kindness and an innocence in her voice that he had rarely ever heard before.

"I suppose I am very big," said Joshua, "and some people have called me a giant."

The dark-haired girl giggled and pointed to the basket full of berries. "We are gathering berries for our mother, Grace," she said laughing. "She and our father, Joseph, are camped down by the Crystal River in Rich Valley. Tonight, our mother is going to make pies with the berries we gather. Do you like pie?" she asked Joshua.

Joshua felt such a wonder and delight at the conversation he was having. He had talked to no one but animals for so long, he hesitated now to speak.

At last he answered, "I love pie. In fact, I love almost any kind of food."

Now the girl with the golden hair smiled at Joshua and pointed to the dark-haired girl. "This is my sister, Hope, and my name is Faith. What is your name?" she asked.

"My father, Jacob, named me Joshua," he told Faith and Hope. "He told me my name meant 'to save,' and that he called me that because I saved him from sorrow and loneliness after his wife and son died."

Then Joshua began to explain how he had been adopted by Jacob after his own family had all died from the terrible fever that swept through Dark River Valley where he had been born. He told about his long journey over Snow Mountain to reach Rich Valley only to find that all the people in Rich Valley were frightened of him because of the Evil Wizard's curse of fear. Faith and Hope listened quietly as Joshua told them all about his life. Finally, Joshua finished his story and asked Faith and Hope, "Why weren't you scared of me like all the other people in Rich Valley?"

Faith and Hope looked at each other and giggled before Faith answered.

"We were in the woods gathering herbs for our mother, Grace. She uses them to help people who are sick get well again. We saw all the animals following you and eating food right out of your hand. They were not afraid of you, and so we knew you were a kind and caring person. That is why we hoped to meet you and find out who you are."

Joshua sat down on the green grass in the clearing and looked in amazement at the two young girls in front of him. He had never heard such compassion and wisdom come from such young children. Most of the children he had known as a child had rejected him, because of his great size. He had felt so isolated and alone as a child that he had feared he would never know friendship with anyone. Now he felt for the first time in his life there was a chance—a chance for understanding and closeness with someone other than just his father.

"Do you think your father and mother might like me?" he asked Faith and Hope.

"Our parents have always been friends to everyone," answered Hope.

"Yes, they are kind to even the people who seem unfriendly" said Faith. "They would love to know a kindhearted person like you."

Joshua felt a sense of peace inside his heart he had never felt before. Here, at last was his chance to have friends and share all his thoughts and dreams with other people. For a moment, Joshua was lost in his thoughts when Hope's voice brought him back from his daydream.

"Why don't you come and meet our parent's tomorrow at our camp beside the Crystal River?" she asked Joshua. "You could eat dinner with us. Our mother loves to have guests for dinner."

"Yes, that would be wonderful," Faith added. "I know Father would enjoy listening to your story."

"I will gladly come and see you and your parent's tomorrow," answered Joshua, "but are you sure they will want me to come?"

"Of course," the girls yelled in unison.

"Don't forget, tomorrow at our camp. It is where Glory Road bends around the Crystal River," said Faith.

Faith and Hope gathered their baskets and began walking back toward Rich Valley. They paused and waved at Joshua at the edge of the clearing.

"Don't forget," yelled Hope as the two girls disappeared into the woods.

"I won't forget," Joshua yelled back. A tear rolled down his face, but Joshua did not want to wipe it away. It was a tear of joy. "I will not forget," he said quietly. "I will never forget this day."

New Friends

Joshua had never been so nervous. It had been a sleepless night, and now the morning sun reminded him a new day was starting. He wondered if Faith and Hope's parents would really like him, or would they fear him, like so many others? *What will happen if they won't even talk to me?* he thought. Joshua's mind went back to his childhood in Dark River Valley. He pictured his father sitting in their home talking to him when he was just a child.

"Remember, Joshua, someday you will find people who will love you for the caring person you are inside," Jacob had said.

Now the moment had come when his father's words might come true. A tiny bird landed on Joshua's shoulder, chirping so Joshua would feed him. Joshua laughed, at least there was someone who enjoyed his company. He gave the little bird some pieces of the berries he had eaten for his own breakfast. The little bird ate them quickly, then flew away. Joshua took a deep breath and started down the trail that led to Crystal River. It was time to see if he could make new friends.

Joseph and Grace took a careful look at the place they had chosen to build their log cabin. It was surrounded by apple trees and one tall oak tree to provide shade. The sound of the Crystal River rushing by made the spot they had picked seem peaceful. All at once Faith and Hope came racing up to their parents with some shiny pebbles they had gathered from the riverbed.

"Look, Mother," said Hope excitedly, "have you ever seen such pretty stones?"

"I don't believe I have," said Grace smiling. "Now, why don't you and Faith help your father gather some wood for a fire. We can fry the fish he caught for dinner."

"Mother, can we have some apple pie after we eat our fish?" asked Faith.

"I declare," said Joseph, "if you girls eat any more apple pie, I think you'll turn into apples."

Hope laughed and started to run toward her father when something in the distance caught her eye. A tall figure was walking quickly toward the family's camp beside the river. His long strides brought him to the camp before anyone had time to guess who it might be. In an instant, Faith and Hope recognized the visitor and ran to greet him.

"Joshua, you came," shouted Faith. "We weren't sure you could find us."

Hope ran and took Joshua's hand and led him to where Joseph and Grace were standing.

"This is my father and mother," said Hope. "We told them all about you."

For a moment, Joseph and Grace stood staring at the largest man either one of them had ever seen. Joshua looked nervously at the two people in front of him, hoping they would not react in fear. Suddenly Joseph stepped forward and took Joshua's hand, shaking it warmly.

"So you are the man the animals trust so much they eat from your bare hands," Joseph said cheerfully. "We are so glad to meet you."

"Yes," said Grace, "come sit down with us. We have been listening to Faith and Hope describe you. We were hoping you would come and visit us."

For a moment, Joshua looked at Faith, Hope, Joseph, and Grace as they all stood together. It was hard to believe an entire family was welcoming him to their camp. And in that instant, he realized that he had at long last found the friends he had always wished for.

The next few hours seemed like only a few minutes to Joshua. He ate the best food he had ever tasted and listened while Joseph and Grace told him about their life on Promise Mountain. Grace told him how her grandmother had taught her about healing and the natural herbs and plants that made people well. It was a skill she had passed on to Faith, who loved to learn about everything. Joseph recounted to Joshua how his father and uncles had taught him about working with wood to build everything imaginable. He showed Joshua a drawing of the cabin he planned to build on the very spot where they now sat around the fire.

After he had listened to their stories, Joshua began to narrate his own story of growing up in Dark River Valley. He told the family about his own father, Jacob, who had taught him how to work with stone to build houses and walls. The afternoon passed quickly as the family and Joshua shared stories about their lives and dreams for the future. Soon the shadows began to gather, and everyone suddenly realized it was almost dark. Joshua rose from his seat and looked toward the path that would take him home.

"I must be getting back to my own camp before dark," he told everyone.

"You must come back soon," cried Faith and Hope together.

"Yes," said Joseph, "perhaps we can teach each other the skills we have learned in making things from wood and stone."

"I see now why Faith and Hope knew you were a kind and gentle man," said Grace. "I hope you will visit us often."

Joshua looked at Faith and Hope chasing butterflies around the camp. The smoke from the campfire slowly curled into the night sky. He turned and looked at Joseph and Grace. He had never met a family like this, but he felt a sense of belonging he had only felt with his own father, Jacob. It was as if he had known this family all his life and not for only a day.

"I hope I can come visit you often," said Joshua. "Thank you for all the things you shared with me today. I think I understand now why Faith and Hope have such kindness deep inside them."

Joshua walked down the trail before turning for a last look back at his new friends. He chuckled to himself as he remembered the words Hope had told her father about the log cabin they would soon build.

"Remember, Father," Hope had told Joseph, "you must build it large enough for Joshua to fit in."

Everyone had laughed, and it was in that moment that Joshua realized this had been one of the happiest days of his life.

Changes

No one in Rich Valley had ever seen a log cabin like the one being built by the new family from Promise Mountain. It was three times the size of any cabin in Rich Valley. However, it was not just the size of the cabin that made it unique. Every log for the new cabin was carved and fitted to the other logs like a giant piece of artwork. Not a single person in Rich Valley could recall watching a carpenter with the skill and artistry of Joseph. People from one end of Rich Valley to the other came to watch Joseph's craftsmanship as he slowly constructed the splendid new house for his family. Yet it was not Joseph's craftsmanship alone that caused so many people to come and witness the grand construction of the new cabin. The man helping Joseph build his grand cabin was someone a few of the people in the valley had seen before.

It was the giant so many of them had run away from when he first entered the valley. Now they watched as the huge man picked up and carried heavy logs that would have taken four or five normal men to lift. Many of the people that came to watch the fascinating construction were still a little bit frightened of Joseph's huge helper. He was, after all, the largest, most powerful person they had ever seen.

They probably would have remained nervous, except for something they witnessed, which left them more amused than afraid. Whenever there was a break in building the cabin, the giant would play some type of child's game with two little girls. When the people saw Faith, Hope, and Joshua play tag or hide-and-seek, they quickly realized that the giant was a gentle soul who laughed and loved just like they did. It wasn't long before the children from all over the valley joined in playing with Faith, Hope, and the "Giant" that had previously terrified everyone. People now laughed as Joshua tried to hide his huge frame when the children played hide-and-seek. Of course, he could hardly find anything large enough to hide behind, but it did not keep him from trying. Slowly, as the people in the valley watched

Joseph and Joshua work together, they realized the deep friendship and bond the two men had. It was as if they had known each other all their life. Joseph was an expert with any type of wood, and Joshua was equally expert with any type of stone. Together they were learning each other's skills and crafting a cabin like no one in the valley had ever seen. There were other things that also drew the community of Rich Valley to the building site of the impressive cabin being constructed by Joseph and Joshua.

Joseph's wife, Grace, was becoming well known for her ability to heal the sick. Her knowledge of herbs and medicines had people from every part of Rich Valley, and the surrounding areas, seeking her help to regain their health. One young mother who had been sick for many years could not believe how much Grace's treatments had helped her.

"It is so good to feel well again," she declared to all those around her.

It wasn't long before crowds of people gathered at the new family's building site to enjoy all the activities that seemed to arise on a daily basis. Some came to see if Grace could help them overcome some type of illness. Some came to see the skills of Joseph and Joshua as they constructed the magnificent cabin. Still others came to listen to Hope sing songs, while Faith played the wooden flute Joseph had crafted for her. Families began to bring food to share with their neighbors, and the gatherings quickly became a kind of community fellowship. The men pitched in and began helping Joseph and Joshua build the splendid cabin. The women helped prepare the food and watched their children play games. When the work was finished, everyone stayed to share the food, music, and tall tales that made even the grumpy people laugh.

The people in Rich Valley were changing. Little by little the spirit of fright, which had gripped the valley for so long, was leaving. The powerful spell of fear the Evil Wizard had put on the people of Rich Valley was disappearing, like a puff of smoke carried away by the wind.

The new attitudes taking shape in Rich Valley were not going unnoticed. High above the valley, a huge raven perched himself in the branches of a dead pine tree. He had been trained by the Evil Wizard to spy on the people in Rich Valley. As he flew back and forth across the valley, he saw the changes the Wizard had trained him to look for.

People were gathering in crowds to share food, love, and laughter. The spirit of fear and distrust was becoming harder and harder to find. Neighbors shared a closeness with each other that had not been felt in many years.

The raven knew his evil master would not be happy with the transformation taking place. He watched the crowds of people singing songs, as their children played on the banks of the Crystal River. He saw the community coming together to help their neighbors in need. The spirit of fear was being replaced by trust and confidence in themselves and in each other.

The raven knew it was time for the Evil Wizard to know what was happening. He was quite certain his evil master would not want Rich Valley to become a place of peace and harmony.

"Caw, caw," he cried as he flew from his dead branch toward Ice Mountain.

His cries echoed through the valley as his huge wings carried him to his destination. His cries had a lonesome, forsaken sound to them as they echoed off the mountain walls.

In a short while, the Evil Wizard would learn his curse of fear had been rejected in Rich Valley. The people of Rich Valley had rediscovered the joy of sharing life and love with each other. The inhabitants of the valley, who now sang songs and laughed and loved, were not aware they had been spied upon. All too soon they would have to face the revenge the Wizard had in store for them.

An Evil Plan

The Wizard's evil helper had never seen his master so angry. When the raven finished his report to the Wizard, a fierce anger seemed to take over the Wizard's entire body. His face became so red and hot, it appeared he might burst into flames any second. Small puffs of smoke came out both his ears. His helper trembled in fear at the sight of his master's fierce anger. It was almost as if a fire of hate and anger was burning inside the Evil Wizard's body.

"So, they have done away with my curse of fear," the Wizard shouted at the mountains. "And now the raven says they are singing and laughing at their stupid gatherings," the Wizard continued to rant.

For several hours, the Wizard continued to rage over the raven's news of peace and goodwill in Rich Valley. His evil helper hid in a closet, hoping his evil master's fiery rage would cool. After a few hours passed, the Evil Wizard emerged from his fit of anger and sat quietly outside, staring off into the distance. His evil helper gathered his courage and approached his evil master cautiously.

"My lord," he said timidly, "what will you now do to the people of Rich Valley, seeing that they have broken your spell?"

At first, the Wizard did not seem to hear his evil servant. A few minutes passed, and then a smile crossed the Wizard's face as though he was having a vision or dream that pleased him.

"I will cause them to fear one final time, and then I will destroy their cursed lives in that valley," replied the Wizard.

"Master, I know you have great powers, but how will you accomplish such a thing?" asked the evil helper.

"Bring me my Book of Spells and Curses from the attic," ordered the Wizard. The Wizard's helper quickly retrieved the huge book and handed it to the Wizard.

"In a few days, I will cast my most evil spell on Snow Mountain from the Book of Spells and Curses. The curse will cause it to snow without stopping for thirty days and thirty nights. When the curse is complete, there will be enough snow on Snow Mountain to bury all of Rich Valley in deep snow," declared the Wizard.

"But how will that harm the people who live in Rich Valley?" asked the evil helper.

The Evil Wizard once again smiled as he envisioned his scheme taking place.

"As the snow gathers on the top of Snow Mountain, I will cast spells on the mountain, which will cause it to begin shaking and trembling. At the end of thirty days, I will cast one last spell, which will make the mountain quake like never before. When Snow Mountain quakes and shudders the final time, the snow will come down in the form of a great avalanche. It will destroy everything in its path. The entire valley will be buried in snow," chuckled the Evil Wizard. "The people will be trapped inside their cabins by the snow. They will starve or come close to starving while they wait for the snow to melt."

"But, master," said the evil helper, "how will the people fear something they do not know will happen? You do want them to fear their doom before it actually happens, don't you?" asked the evil servant.

"They will know it is coming because someone will warn them about the great avalanche that is going to occur. They will be warned many days before I cast the final curse on Snow Mountain. They will know their destruction is coming, and they will fear as they have never feared before," said the Wizard as a cruel smile spread over his face.

The evil servant thought about his master's plan for a moment. "I do not understand who will warn them," said the evil helper. "No one in Rich Valley knows anything about an avalanche. Who will warn them about an avalanche that will destroy their valley?"

The Wizard turned and looked into his evil helper's eyes. "You will," said the wicked Wizard. "You will go disguised as a helpful traveler and warn them about everything that is to happen. Then they will live in terror for many days before their destruction comes."

The Wizard sat back with an evil grin on his face. He seemed satisfied with his plan of revenge against the people of Rich Valley. For a moment, there was complete silence, as though the wizard's vicious plans had removed all life from the surroundings.

Finally, the Evil Wizard's helper broke the silence. "And what will happen when all the snow that buries Rich Valley starts to melt?" he inquired.

At this the Wizard jumped up laughing, as though he were celebrating a great victory.

"The melted snow will flood the valley and destroy their homes and crops. Anyone left alive will be without food or shelter. They will be doomed," the Wizard shouted in glee. "It is the perfect plan."

The Evil Wizard sat back, happily imagining the destruction of Rich Valley, while his cruel assistant began packing his bags. A visitor to the Wizard's home would have marveled how the Wizard and his helper only found happiness in the misery of others. It seemed the destruction of people was the only thing they could ever celebrate.

The evil helper began to think about the task he had to perform. It would not be long before he would enter Rich Valley, pretending to be a helpful traveler. He would assure the people he was only there to warn them of the terrible avalanche shortly to come. He had been well trained by the Wizard in the art of fooling people. There was no doubt the Evil Wizard was the master of deception. The Wizard's accomplice would have no difficulty pretending to be concerned about the tragedy that awaited the people in the valley. Then he could gleefully watch as the people descended back into the fear and terror they had known before. It was a magnificent, monstrous plan.

Far away, the people of Rich Valley once again gathered to share and appreciate the joys of friendship and love. The sounds of their joyful fellowship filled the air in Rich Valley. It was the sound of people who once again had discovered the pleasures of sharing life. Little did they know the wickedness that would soon approach Rich Valley.

Courage or Fear

It was a rare thing to see all the people in Rich Valley gathered in one place. To most people in the crowd, it looked like every man, woman, and child in the valley and surrounding areas were assembled in Spirit Meadow. It was unusual to see so many people in Spirit Meadow. Usually the meadow was occupied only by prairie dogs and ground squirrels that built their homes there. The green meadow was at the bottom of Snow Mountain and just before the widest road leading to Rich Valley. It had been given its name by the first settlers to Rich Valley because they believed some merciful spirit had led them to such a beautiful place. Now the people had congregated in the grassy meadow to discuss the news that had caused so many of them to be afraid.

A stranger had arrived in Rich Valley three days ago and had begun telling the people some troubling information. It appeared as if the snowfall on Snow Mountain had caused more snow to gather there than at any time in the history of the valley. This was not the only disturbing report that had upset so many of the citizens. The stranger had also reported that small tremors had caused the great mountain to shake and tremble. No one could remember such tremors on Snow Mountain, and the people now wondered what would become of their beautiful valley.

The helpful traveler, who had spread the news, was someone none of them had ever seen before. He appeared to be greatly concerned about their welfare, and the people eagerly thanked him for his information. His prediction of a great avalanche was perhaps the most troubling news of all. When his reporting had spread throughout the valley, ten brave men had climbed Snow Mountain to see if it was all true. They had returned with heartbreaking news for the people of Rich Valley. There was indeed more snow on Snow Mountain than any of them had ever seen. Not only that, but the mountain tremors had become so powerful that even in Spirit Meadow the people felt the ground shaking beneath their feet.

The spirit of fear that had ruled the valley for so long seemed to grip their lives once again. The helpful stranger repeated his warning about the great avalanche and then watched as the huge crowd of people talked nervously about their future. The Evil Wizard's assistant, who had pretended to be a helpful stranger, now left the crowd and began his journey back to Ice Mountain.

"They are so easily misled," he said to himself. "The Wizard will laugh when I tell him how easily I convinced them I was their friend."

He was sure the Wizard would appreciate his efforts in scaring the people of Rich Valley. The spirit of fear now returned as people imagined the gigantic avalanche that would soon destroy Rich Valley. Before long, the Wizard could return in person to see the effects of the great avalanche he would create from his home on Ice Mountain. Then the Evil Wizard and his helper would celebrate as never before. The evil assistant took one last look back at Rich Valley. He was confident that in a little while the entire valley would panic. The Wizard's evil helper smiled. It was always easy to mislead people who trusted their neighbors and friends. Their faith in the goodness of others made them so easy to deceive. They believed he was just a kind traveler warning them for their own protection.

"What fools they are," he chuckled to himself gleefully.

Now he would travel swiftly to Ice Mountain and help the Wizard make the final preparations for the destruction of Rich Valley. He could hardly wait for the final curse to trigger the massive avalanche that would destroy the valley. These people that had dared go against the Evil Wizard's curse of fear would soon learn a lesson they would never forget.

As the Evil Wizard's assistant left for Ice Mountain, another unique soul completed his own expedition. Something had compelled the old stone mason from Dark River Valley to make the nearly impossible journey over Snow Mountain. His heart had told him that he must find his long-lost son. Now he seemed very tired as he descended from Snow Mountain and headed for Rich Valley. The long, dangerous journey from his home had been a severe challenge for the determined traveler. The trip over Snow Mountain had been especially difficult, because of the tremendous amount of snow that had fallen on the mountain. The elderly man had also struggled with the ground shaking beneath his feet as he finished the final part of his expedition. He was not sure exactly what was happening on Snow Mountain. In his lifetime, he had never heard of tremors or huge amounts of snow on the mountain. He sat down briefly and caught his breath before heading toward the crowd of people he saw gathered in a nearby meadow.

When some of the people in the crowd saw the old man, they ran to help him. They could see he had just come from Snow Mountain, and they marveled at the idea he had accomplished such a difficult journey. One woman brought him some bread and soup, while a young man started a small fire so the elderly gentleman could warm himself.

"I am so grateful to find such help," the old man said smiling. "I wonder if anyone here has, perhaps, seen my son."

The small group that had collected around the old man looked at each other.

"What is the name of your son?" a woman asked the elderly man.

"He is called Joshua," said the old man, "and I am his father, Jacob, from Dark River Valley."

All at once the entire crowd gathered in Spirit Meadow began surrounding Jacob.

"Your son built the fireplace in my cabin," said one man.

"He saved my little daughter from drowning in the Crystal River," said another.

One after another told Jacob about all the good things Joshua had done for the people in Rich Valley. The old man was overwhelmed by emotion. He had never imagined that Joshua would touch the lives of so many people. Jacob wiped several tears from his eyes and tried to regain his composure. Joshua had found a place where people had realized what a kind, compassionate man he really was. It was all Jacob had ever hoped for and more than he ever thought possible.

Suddenly the sea of people parted, and a huge pair of hands gently held the old man in an embrace.

"My beloved son," was all that Jacob could say.

For a long time, Joshua held his father closely, as both men felt the warmth of each other's love. A few moments passed while they each relished the moment of seeing each other again. Then they sat by the fire and began to share all the news they had not shared in so long.

Out of the crowd of people, Joseph, Grace, Faith, and Hope appeared, and Joshua quickly introduced Jacob to all of them.

"You and Joshua must spend the night with us," insisted Grace. "I know you must be hungry and tired from your journey."

Joshua helped his father to his feet, and they made their way to Joseph's almost completed cabin. Jacob marveled at the splendid cabin, and the rest of the night was spent eating and sharing every bit of news that had transpired in the last year.

Finally Jacob said, "I could never have imagined my son finding such a wonderful family or place as this. Tomorrow we will talk some more, but I am so weary I must now rest."

"Don't you want to play some games before you sleep?" asked Hope.

Everyone laughed as Grace quickly prepared a place for Jacob to sleep.

"Perhaps tomorrow we can play," answered Jacob, "but I can barely keep my eyes open right now."

Slowly but surely, everyone found a bed and drifted off to sleep. It had been a long day for all of them, and there would be much more to do tomorrow.

Morning found Spirit Meadow again full of people trying to decide what they could do to save themselves and their homes. The people argued back and forth as the spirit of fear and distrust once again gained foothold among them. After a while, Jacob rose and asked the crowd if he could speak.

The people fell silent, and Jacob began to address the crowd, "People of Rich Valley, I know what it is to face fear. Long ago, in Dark River Valley, where I am from, a terrible fever swept through my homeland and killed my wife and baby boy. I was broken, and then someone brought me a child, whose family had also died from the fever. It was Joshua. As I looked at this baby boy, I had to make a choice. I could live in fear and despair, or I could fight my fear and try to live with courage. When this child smiled at me, I knew I must live with courage. It is better to live one day with courage than a thousand years in fear. Fear has robbed you for many years of the joy life should bring. When you found your courage, you began once again to share life and laughter and joy. You cannot return now to a life of fear and sadness. Face this trouble with bravery and boldness. It is the only way to have a chance at victory."

For a few minutes, the crowd was silent, and then they began whispering among themselves.

"What can we do to stop the great avalanche?" shouted a woman in the crowd.

"It seems hopeless," cried a young woman holding her young baby.

Joseph held up his hands for silence, then turned and looked at Jacob.

"What can we do, Jacob, to stop the great avalanche from destroying our valley?" he asked.

Jacob took a stick and began making a line in the dirt. The line went all the way across Spirit Meadow to the entrance to Rich Valley.

"I am a builder, as is my beloved son, Joshua. With your help, we can build a great wall of stone and mortar along this line. If we build it tall enough, and strong enough, it can stop the great avalanche from destroying Rich Valley," said Jacob.

The crowd took a moment to realize what Jacob was suggesting.

"But it might fail," said an older man in the crowd.

"Yes," said Jacob, "it might fail, but I would rather try and fail than live in fear and do nothing."

Suddenly Joshua walked over to a huge rock sitting at the edge of Snow Mountain. With a great effort, he picked the rock up and carried it to the line Jacob had drawn in the dirt.

"This is the first stone for the great wall, Father. I am ready to help you build the wall to save our valley," said Joshua.

Joseph quickly followed Joshua's example and took up a heavy rock, which he placed beside the one Joshua had laid.

"I will also help you build the wall, Jacob," cried Joseph.

All at once, the entire group of people gathered in Spirit Meadow seemed inspired by a feeling of daring. Somehow a spirit of bravery had taken over the people gathered in Spirit Meadow. One by one, they began encouraging one another to fight to save their homes and their beautiful valley. Frowns and tears were now replaced by smiles and a bold determination. The spirit of fear, which had threatened to defeat them only moments before, had been crushed. The first part of the battle to save Rich Valley had been fought in the minds of the people. The spirit of courage had won.

The Wall

No one in Rich Valley had ever seen someone work like Joshua. For weeks, the giant man had carried huge rocks to build the wall, hardly taking even a moment to rest. He was not alone in his efforts to build the wall. Every man, woman, and child in Rich Valley knew their homes and lives could be destroyed by a great avalanche.

It had been almost a month now since the visiting traveler had warned the people of a huge avalanche likely to come from Snow Mountain. From that moment until now, everyone had worked hard to try and save their beautiful valley. It was more than just saving their cabins or belongings; it was saving a way of life they had built together over the years.

The men had helped Joshua carry the heavy rocks that anchored the wall and gave it strength. The women had worked gathering clay and mortar that held the rocks together to make the wall sturdy. Jacob had even been assisted by the older children mixing the mortar and clay to hold the rocks in place. Day after day, the entire population had worked side by side, hoping they could stop the avalanche that had been predicted. At night, the people would go home exhausted from the work, only to rise the next day, ready to work again.

Grace could not believe the determination of the people she had come to know. One day she turned to Jacob and asked, "Jacob, why do these people work so hard day after day? What drives them to do such difficult work?"

Jacob looked out at the people working hand in hand to save their valley.

"It is love," Jacob replied.

For a moment, Grace seemed puzzled by Jacob's answer.

"I'm not sure I understand, Jacob," said Grace. "Did you say *love*?"

Jacob turned and smiled at Grace.

He spoke softly now, almost in a hushed whisper, "Yes, I said *love*, Grace. It was love that caused these people to build their homes in this valley. The love of the beauty the valley held. It was love that made them have families so they could share the wonder of it. It was love that made them work together to give their children a future. Now it is love that drives them to save what they know it so valuable."

Grace looked out over the valley and then at the people working with one another to construct the wall.

"I never thought of it that way, Jacob," said Grace, "but I believe you are right. I have only lived here a little while, and I have already come to love this valley and its people."

Joseph approached Jacob and Grace and sat down wearily beside them.

"I have never worked so hard in all my life," he said to them both, "but I think everyone in this valley has outworked me."

Jacob and Grace both laughed as Joseph lay on the ground catching his breath. The sun was going down, and it was almost time to quit for the day.

"Jacob, do you think the wall will really stop the great avalanche from destroying Rich Valley?" asked Joseph.

"I do not know, but it will not be long before we will find out," said Jacob.

"How do you know it will be soon?" asked Joseph.

"The animals are beginning to leave Snow Mountain and looking for new places to find shelter," said Jacob. "That means our time to build the wall is almost gone."

Joseph looked at Jacob with a somewhat puzzled expression. "What makes you think the animals leaving Snow Mountain means an avalanche is soon to come Jacob?" asked Joseph.

"The animals are leaving Snow Mountain because they know some type of great destruction is coming in a very short while. They feel things, and know things, that we as humans do not. They feel the earth moving and know they must flee from the devastation that is soon to happen. The animals always have a story to tell, if you know how to listen."

Jacob paused for a moment, then looked in the distance toward Snow Mountain.

"We have worked to build the wall for nearly a month now, and it is almost finished. Tomorrow we will set poles as braces to the wall to make it even stronger. Then we must wait and see if it will save Rich Valley or not," Jacob concluded.

The sound of laughter broke the somber moment as Faith and Hope joined their parents and Jacob.

"We have been taking water to all the people who were working," announced Hope.

"Yes, and we helped Joshua find some more big rocks for the wall," added Faith.

"Did you help him carry them?" asked Grace.

"No, Mother," said Hope, "they are much too heavy for us to lift. Only Joshua can carry such heavy rocks."

Just then Joshua joined the group and laid down tiredly. "The wall is nearly eight feet tall now," he announced to Jacob, "and it covers the entire opening to Rich Valley."

Jacob looked fondly at his son and then turned to watch the setting sun in the distance.

"You have worked hard, Joshua, but tomorrow will be our last day to work on the wall," said Jacob. "Then we must stand back and see if our labors can hold back the great force that nature seems ready to send our way."

The sound of thunder came from Snow Mountain, and everyone turned to look at the distant mountain in the last light of sunset.

"I had a dream about the mountain last night," said Faith.

"What was your dream, Faith?" asked Grace gently.

"I dreamed there were a hundred white horses gathered on top of Snow Mountain. They were powerful and strong, and it seemed like they were waiting to come down from the mountain. Then something happened I could not see, and they came charging down, as if nothing could ever stop them," finished Faith.

"And then what happened?" asked Joshua.

"A man stood at the bottom of Snow Mountain, as if he was waiting for them. I thought the sun must be shining on him, because he was very bright. He held up his hand for the horses to stop, and I wondered if they would run over him and trample him to death," said Faith.

Everyone now looked at Faith as she took a deep breath.

"What happened, Faith, how did your dream end?" asked Joseph anxiously.

"I woke up, because I smelled the bread Mother was baking for our breakfast," answered Faith. "I do not know what became of all the horses."

Everyone laughed as some of the stress from the past few weeks seemed lifted away by Faith's story.

"Faith has always been our dreamer," explained Grace, as she looked fondly upon her daughter.

"It was a good dream, Faith," said Jacob. "Perhaps the white horses will obey the shiny man's signal."

Grace held Faith in her arms, while Joseph picked up Hope, who had fallen fast asleep.

"It is time for us all to go to the cabin and sleep," said Joseph. "We have one final day's work to complete the wall tomorrow."

"Yes," whispered Joshua to himself, "one last chance to finish our work before the white horses come charging down."

It was growing dark on Ice Mountain as the Evil Wizard studied his Book of Spells and Curses. He thought for a moment about the people in Rich Valley and the terror they were probably feeling. He was confident his evil assistant had done a good job of alarming the people about the approaching avalanche. *They will certainly be paralyzed with fear*, he thought as he smiled.

Just then his evil helper entered the room with wood for the fireplace. As he put wood on the fire, he turned and looked at his wicked master studying his Book of Spells and Curses.

"Master, it has been thirty days now since I warned the people in Rich Valley about the avalanche," he said. "When will you cast the final curse so it will happen?"

The Evil Wizard turned toward the fireplace and watched as the flames began to burn the new wood.

"Tomorrow night at midnight, I will pronounce the final curse on Rich Valley. The people will be in their homes when they hear the great roar of the avalanche coming. Their homes will be buried in snow so deep they cannot leave them. Their precious cabins will become their tombs," concluded the Wizard.

"What if the snow melts, and they are able to escape their cabins?" inquired the evil assistant.

At this, the Evil Wizard laughed out loud, as if relishing the panic, he was sure the people would feel.

"Those who do not starve to death trapped inside their cabin will live the rest of their life in fear," said the Wizard. "They will become as lifeless as those who died."

Once more, the Wizard turned and watched the flames of the fire. He often thought about the ability of the fire to give warmth and light, then turn and destroy so completely.

"And what will we do after you deliver the final curse?" asked the evil assistant.

The Wizard rose from the table and walked toward the door of his home. The darkness had fallen on Ice Mountain, and a freezing wind was blowing.

"We will take a journey to Rich Valley and see all the destruction the avalanche has brought. Then we will gather the people left alive and tell them this is the penalty for defying my curse of fear. They will never dare to hope or sing or dream good things ever again. Then we will return to Ice Mountain and celebrate their misery," finished the Wizard.

"It will be a fitting revenge for their rebellion against your curse of fear," said the evil helper.

The Wizard's face darkened as he looked once more into the fire. "Yes," he said slowly, "a very fitting revenge indeed."

The Avalanche

Joshua lifted the heavy log and placed it into the hole Joseph had dug for it. The two men then worked together to fasten it to the wall as a brace to make the wall even stronger. Jacob looked at the wall, which now stretched all the way from one end of Spirit Meadow to the other. He nodded in approval. The stone wall was almost eight feet tall now and completely blocked the main entrance into Rich Valley. The wooden braces designed by Joseph had added a great deal of strength to the wall, and it was, by all accounts, an impressive structure.

"It is finished," Jacob said simply as he completed his inspection of the construction.

"I cannot believe we completed such a great wall in less than thirty days of work," declared Joseph.

"Nor can I," agreed Joshua, "but there it stands, whether we believe it or not."

"It is amazing what people can accomplish when they work together and are determined," Jacob stated. "I would not have thought it possible to build such a structure in such a short time, but I have seen impossible things happen before. The people of Rich Valley have worked a great work to save their valley. Now we can only hope the wall will accomplish its purpose."

Jacob raised a bugle Joseph had fashioned from a cow's horn and blew on it with all his might. It had become the signal for the people of the valley to gather each day as they prepared to work on the wall. The sound echoed throughout the valley, and the people from every corner of the valley headed toward the sound.

"What are you going to tell the people?" asked Joseph as he and Joshua finished gathering their tools.

"It is time to tell them what they must do to prepare for the great avalanche that is almost certain to come," answered Jacob. "We must also encourage their spirits so that they do not give up the hope they have found in working together to save this valley."

The people of Rich Valley slowly gathered in the yard of Sarah, the dressmaker of Rich Valley. Sarah's cabin was the closest home to Spirit Meadow and had been where the people gathered each morning as they prepared to work on the wall. Her home stood only a few yards from where Joshua and Joseph had placed the last wooden brace on the wall. Now, with all the people assembled, Jacob began to speak.

"You have accomplished a marvelous work in building this wall to save your lives and your homes in this valley. Even as we stand here, we can feel Snow Mountain shaking, and we know the great avalanche may come any moment. Here is what you must do to prepare for your safety. Take all the food you can gather and put it inside your cabins. Those of you who are younger must help the older people collect the food they need for their homes. If the wall fails and your home is buried in snow, the food you store will keep you alive until the snow melts."

"And what if the snow doesn't melt before our food runs out?" asked Aaron, the farmer.

"You will do everything you can to survive. You might even have to dig your way out of the snow," answered Jacob.

The people began to talk among themselves. Joseph heard the anxiety in their voices and held up his hands.

"Good people of Rich Valley, you have come together and built a great wall to save your lives and the lives of your neighbors. You have worked together, lived together, fellowshipped together, and fought together to fulfill your dreams. Whatever happens in the next few hours, you will once again work together to preserve your lives and the lives of those you care about. Do not give up your hope in this difficult hour."

The people listened carefully to Joseph. They had come to respect him, because he, Grace, Faith, and Hope had helped so many people in the valley.

"We should begin to gather all the food we need before the light of the day is gone and the darkness comes," said Aaron.

"Don't anyone forget to collect food for the older people," reminded Sarah.

The people slowly broke up into groups and began gathering the food to store in their cabins. Many of the people helped Grace, Faith, Hope, and Joseph round up all the food they could find for the older people in the valley. Jacob and Joshua walked back to the wall to make their final inspection.

"We have made a strong wall, Father," said Joshua. "I believe it will stand against even a great avalanche."

Jacob smiled at his son. "I have always trusted your judgment, Joshua. Even as a young boy, you were wiser than most grown-ups. I pray now that you are right once again."

With the remaining hours of daylight, the people of Rich Valley prepared for the great avalanche they were certain would come very soon. Every effort was made to ensure the weakest among them was provided for. As the sun slowly set in the distance, the people embraced their neighbors and friends, not knowing what the night might bring.

Faith and Hope ran to each person they could find to pass out all the berries and nuts they had gathered that afternoon. Grace stood back admiring her daughters. There was a giving nature in both of them that seemed almost sacred in her eyes.

With the sun now gone, all the families of Rich Valley entered their homes and began the long wait until morning. For many, it would not be the usual night of restful sleep. The thought of a great avalanche of snow bearing down on the valley was troubling to the minds of many. The doors of all the homes in Rich Valley were closed and fastened, and a quiet darkness settled on the valley.

The same darkness also came to Ice Mountain, but the Evil Wizard did not mind the darkness at all. The darkness of his heart seemed to be more than comfortable with the darkness of the night. The Wizard sat alone in the dimness of his home whispering an odd phrase.

"Mortisque timores dabo," he repeated over and over. It was an ancient phrase from his Book of Spells and Curses.

For hours, the Wizard sat quietly repeating the phrase until his evil assistant entered the dark room.

"My lord," asked the evil helper, "what does 'Mortisque timores dabo' mean?"

"It is a language I learned long ago when I first began to study the Book of Spells and Curses," the Wizard answered. "It means, 'I give you fear and death.'"

The evil assistant shuddered. There were times that the darkened mind of his master frightened even him.

The Wizard rose as his clock struck midnight. He pointed his finger south toward Rich Valley.

"Mortisque timores dabo," he shouted at the top of his lungs. Then he clasped his hands together and pointed menacingly toward Snow Mountain. "Mortisque timores dabo," he shouted once more into the darkness.

The Evil Wizard sat down exhausted. The casting of the final curse had taken all his strength. "We can rest now," he told his evil assistant. "The people of Rich Valley will now meet their fate."

Sarah sat down and lit a single candle on the table she used to make clothes. She had been a dressmaker since her mother had taught her the art of weaving as a young child. She loved to make beautiful things for people to wear. It was her chief pleasure in life to see people so happy when she showed them new clothes, she had made for them. Now she sat alone in her cabin trembling. She was frightened at the idea of a great avalanche crashing down the mountain. Would the wall they had built hold it back? She knew that a large part of her fear was not knowing what would happen next. She looked at the bowl of berries and nuts Faith and Hope had left for her on the table.

"If I am to die, at least my final memory will be an act of kindness," she said to herself.

A few hours passed, and Sarah finally drifted off to a troubled sleep, alone in her cabin. At midnight, she awoke to what seemed to be the sound of a great thunder rolling down Snow Mountain. Louder and louder the sound grew as the avalanche came crashing down the mountain. Giant pine trees snapped like twigs from the force of the great avalanche. Sarah covered her ears and fell to the floor of the cabin crying. The roar of the avalanche was a terrifying noise to all who heard it. The sound continued for what seemed like an eternity. Then suddenly, all was quiet. Sarah got up slowly in the darkness. She lit the candle that had burned out and looked around the cabin. Everything seemed in place, but she wondered if her cabin was now buried deep in the snows of the great avalanche. *There is nothing I can do before the light of the coming day*, she thought. She crawled into her bed and pulled the blankets over her head, as if to hide from the dread she felt.

"What will tomorrow bring?" she said to the darkness, and then she fell asleep.

The darkness of the night slowly passed, and the sun rose once again to the beauty of Rich Valley. Across the valley, families awoke wondering what the night had brought. In her little cabin, close to the wall, Sarah slept uneasily in the early hours of the morning.

"Sarah, Sarah, please open the door," shouted a voice.

Sarah rubbed her eyes, but she could see nothing in the darkness of the small cabin. "I must have been dreaming," she said to herself and turned over to go asleep again.

A knock on the door woke Sarah once again, and she lit a candle to see her way to the door. For just a moment, she worried that the snow burying her cabin would come inside when she opened the door. Then it quickly occurred to her that if someone was knocking on her door, she was not buried in snow as she had imagined. Sarah opened the door cautiously, nevertheless, and there stood Faith, Hope, and Joshua smiling at her, as if they had just found a treasure.

"Sarah," shouted Faith, "come outside and see."

"Hurry, Sarah," yelled Hope, "you must come and see everything."

Sarah quickly dressed and stepped outside into the bright sunshine. Several rabbits, eating some of her garden vegetables, ran away quickly, as if they knew they had committed some crime.

"We knew your cabin was close to the wall and that you were worried about the avalanche," explained Joshua. "At first light, we came to check on you first."

Now Sarah ran to Faith and Hope and hugged them both tightly. She could not help but cry a few tears of relief knowing now the danger had passed.

"But what about the great avalanche?" she asked Joshua. "I heard it come in the night, and it sounded so powerful. I imagined the whole valley would be buried in snow."

"Come see," said Joshua simply.

Joshua, Faith, Hope, and Sarah now walked rapidly to the wall. There it stood. Sarah stared at the wall that had almost a foot of snow above the top of it. Some of the snow had come over the top and lay harmlessly in piles next to the wall. Faith and Hope ran to the piles and began making a snowman.

"It held," whispered Sarah. "It held," she shouted. "It held."

Now she ran to Faith and Hope and began helping them make the snowman. A combination of joy, relief, and happiness flooded her soul.

Across the entire length of the wall, the people of Rich Valley had emerged from their homes and now began examining the results of the great avalanche they had heard come during the night.

"We're saved," shouted one old man. He grabbed his wife and began dancing back and forth in front of the wall.

His wife protested for a moment, then abandoned her embarrassment, and began dancing with him in celebration.

Gradually, the entire population of Rich Valley began congregating at the wall. Some climbed ladders to the top and looked at Spirit Meadow on the other side of the wall they had built.

"It is like a lake of snow," yelled one man.

"A valley of snow," marveled another. "In all my life I have never seen so much snow in one place."

As the people assembled at the wall and celebrated their deliverance from the destruction of the great avalanche, they were joined by Jacob, Joseph, and Grace. Many of the people ran to Jacob and began to thank him for his help in saving Rich Valley.

"How will you celebrate today, Jacob?" asked Sarah. "Now that you have helped save our valley."

Jacob paused for a moment as he looked over all the people that had come to the wall.

"I would like to go to the road your ancestors first built when they came and established Rich Valley. I believe you call it Glory Road," said Jacob.

"Yes, that is its name," answered Sarah. "But why do you want to go there?" she asked.

"I want to walk down the same path my son Joshua walked down when he first came to Rich Valley. There is something there he has told me about. I should like to see it for myself," said Jacob.

Many of the people saw Jacob, Joshua, Joseph, Grace, Faith, Hope, and Sarah walking toward Glory Road and began to join them. Soon most of the inhabitants of Rich Valley found themselves congregated at the start of Glory Road.

"Now, Jacob, tell us why you wanted to come to Glory Road," said Sarah.

Jacob stood on top of a large, flat rock that marked the beginning of Glory Road and begin to speak.

"When I first came to Rich Valley, my son, Joshua, told me about his first experience here. He told me that everyone feared him as he walked from one end of the valley to the other. After he had walked through the entire valley, he came to a great, tall pine tree with a curse carved into it by an Evil Wizard who had visited the valley. The curse read:

PEOPLE OF RICH VALLEY, MY WORDS YOU SHALL HEAR
THE WORDS I WILL SPEAK, WHICH WILL CAUSE YOU TO FEAR
JOY INTO SORROW, AND LAUGHTER TO TEARS
YOU WILL ALWAYS BE AFRAID FOR ALL OF YOUR YEARS

"Joseph also told me about coming to this valley and seeing this horrible curse carved upon this grand old tree. I have been in your beautiful valley now for over a month, but I have not yet had time to see the Evil Wizard's curse carved upon this majestic pine tree. Now that you have fought against the spirit of fear, I would like to see this magnificent tree. Perhaps the curse of fear carved into its trunk can now be removed," finished Jacob.

The people continued down Glory Road until they all arrived at the great pine tree with the Evil Wizard's curse carved upon it.

For a few moments, the people stood silently gazing at the foul curse of fear carved into the great pine tree by the Evil Wizard long ago.

"Jacob, do you think the great avalanche was part of the curse?" asked Sarah.

"I do not know, Sarah," replied Jacob. "This Evil Wizard certainly hated the people of this valley and intended to destroy them. His curse and his powers are beyond my understanding."

Jacob turned and looked at Joseph and Joshua as they gazed upon the Wizard's engraving.

"I think it is time to remove this dreadful curse from Rich Valley," said Jacob. He turned once more toward Joshua and Joseph. "Perhaps you two would be willing to help take away this evil curse of fear. I think tomorrow morning would be a good time to begin."

"I will gladly join you to do that task, Father," replied Joshua.

"When I first saw this terrible curse, I wanted to take my carpenter's tools and remove it," said Joseph. "Now I am glad the time has come to join you both, and the people of this valley, to erase this curse of fear once and for all."

Jacob nodded in agreement, then turned to the people that had assembled next to the majestic pine tree.

"And what is the will of the people of Rich Valley concerning this curse of fear?" asked Jacob.

The people talked among themselves for a few minutes before Aaron the farmer stood up as their spokesman.

"We have hoped and dreamed that the time would come for the chance to remove the Evil Wizard's curse from our valley. We are thankful for you, Jacob, as well as Joshua and Joseph. You have led us and given us courage to fight against the fear. Our spirits are joined to yours to see this curse removed," said Aaron.

"Then let us return to our homes for now," said Jacob, "and tomorrow, we will join our hearts together and take away this awful curse forever."

So the people quietly began returning to their homes, joyful at their deliverance from the great avalanche, and happy that the terrible curse would finally be removed from their valley.

A Curse Removed

The next morning found Joseph and Faith standing under the great pine tree with the Evil Wizard's curse of fear on it. Joseph looked down at his young daughter and smiled. As Faith had grown older, she insisted on accompanying her father as often as possible when he set out on an important job.

"Father, I do not understand this curse," said Faith. "Why did this Wizard want the people of Rich Valley to be afraid. Didn't he know that would make them feel bad?"

"It is difficult to understand," said Joseph, "but I will try and explain it as best I can. I believe there is a Spirit that created all things in this world. I felt that Spirit when I was a young man and saw all the beautiful things in this world. When you were born, I felt that Spirit in a special, more powerful way. It was as if the Spirit that created all things had touched my spirit. I looked at you, and I felt joy, and I knew that something greater than myself had a part in your coming into this world."

"I know you thank the Spirit that created all things when you pray, Father," said Faith, "and I also have heard you ask for His help when things are troubled."

"That is because I believe the Spirit of creation is a loving Spirit that shows us the way to love others and help them," said Joseph. "That is what I feel when I talk to Him."

Faith looked up at the giant pine tree and quietly read the curse of fear the Wizard had carved into it.

"But, Father, this curse seems to want people to be hurt and afraid. The Spirit that created all things would not want that," declared Faith.

"No, I don't believe He wants such things at all," said Joseph. "There is another spirit at work here. The Spirit that created all things is a Spirit of love and joy and life. The spirit of the Evil Wizard is a dark spirit of anger and hate. The spirit that drives him makes him want to destroy and kill everything that is good."

"I do not like the spirit of the Evil Wizard, Father," said Faith. "Is that why we have come to remove his curse from this tree?"

"Yes, Faith," answered Joseph, "that is exactly why we have come to take away the curse of fear carved into this beautiful tree."

A blue jay landed on a limb of the great pine tree, just above the Evil Wizard's curse. He looked at Faith and Joseph curiously, as if questioning their reason for being there.

Faith laughed and pointed at the colorful bird.

"What a pretty bird, Father," said Faith. "He wants to watch us while you remove the curse from the tree."

Joseph grinned at his daughter. Faith and Hope had added so much to his and Grace's life. It was hard to imagine a life without them.

"He is welcome to watch," said Joseph. "I will try to leave his tree a little more attractive when I am finished."

As Faith and Joseph admired the blue jay, Jacob, Grace, Joshua, and Hope joined the group watching the graceful bird fly from limb to limb in the tall tree.

"It looks like you have an audience for your good work today" said Jacob, as he laughed and shook hands with Joseph.

"I am glad to have an audience to do this task," said Joseph. "It is strange, but I sense the presence of evil any time I go near the Wizard's curse."

"I feel it also, Joseph," answered Jacob. "There is a power to the spirit of darkness that caused this Wizard to hate the people of this valley."

"Jacob, what do you believe about the Spirit that created this world and the spirit of darkness?" asked Joseph.

"I felt the spirit of darkness when my wife and child died of the fever in Dark River Valley long ago," answered Jacob. "I cried out in my anger and grief that the two people I loved most had been taken away from me. The spirit of darkness wanted me to hate and fear. For a moment, I was gripped with hopelessness and fury against everything in creation and the Creator. I fell to my knees in despair and cried out to the Spirit that created this world. It was in that moment that something inside my spirit assured me that my wife and child were with the Spirit that made all things. They were safe with Him, and somehow I would see them again someday."

"And then what did you feel?" asked Joseph.

"I was sorrowful for a long time," answered Jacob, "but there was also a hope inside me, even in my sorrow."

"Is that when someone brought you Joshua?" asked Joseph.

Jacob smiled and looked at Joshua, who was trying to teach Hope and Faith how to carve letters into rock with a hammer and chisel.

"Yes, that is when someone brought me Joshua," said Jacob. "I felt the Spirit of love from the Creator in the moment that I saw him. When I looked at Joshua, it was almost as though I was touching the Spirit that made all things. There was a love inside him, even as a young child, that was greater than in most people."

"We have all grown to love him," said Joseph, "even though we have not known him very long."

Grace approached Jacob and Joseph as they stood at the base of the great pine tree.

"Jacob, do you have any plans for what happens after Joseph removes the curse from this tree?" she asked quietly.

Jacob smiled at Grace and winked at Joseph.

"It sounds like perhaps you have a plan for me, Grace," Jacob said laughing. "After all the wonderful food you have fed me and Joshua, I am sure I cannot refuse your request."

"I am glad to hear you say that," said Grace smiling. "When Joseph has finished removing the Wizard's curse from the pine tree, I would like you to replace it with a blessing."

"What type of blessing would you like, Grace?" asked Jacob.

"A blessing for the people of Rich Valley," Grace answered, "a blessing to take the place of the Evil Wizard's curse of fear."

Jacob looked at Grace fondly. He had grown to admire the young woman's courage and wisdom in the short while they had known each other.

"It is an excellent idea, Grace," exclaimed Jacob. "Where would we put this blessing once I have created it?"

"I was thinking, perhaps, Joshua could engrave it on the large white stone over there where Glory Road ends," said Grace. "A large crowd of people could stand and read it together. It would be a reminder of our deliverance from evil."

Now Joshua, who had overheard Grace's idea, joined Joseph and Jacob as all three of them seemed to ponder Grace's plan together. Finally, Jacob stepped toward Grace, smiling.

"Joshua, Joseph, and I have decided something," said Jacob.

"What have you decided?" asked Grace, with a grin on her face.

"We have decided that most great ideas come from women," said Jacob, "and we would be lost without them."

Everyone laughed and then watched as Joseph gathered his carpenter's tools and walked over to the great pine tree. For a moment, he stood staring at the evil curse.

The tall pine tree swayed slowly in the wind as Jacob, Joshua, Grace, Faith, and Hope all stared at its majestic beauty.

"We are with you, Joseph," said Joshua. "Take away this vile curse from this valley."

"Yes, Father," said Hope, "the tree will be happier when the curse is gone from it."

Joseph smiled at his youngest daughter. He often wondered if his daughters knew how their observations made him consider things more profoundly.

As Joseph began removing the Evil Wizard's curse from the majestic pine tree, Joshua and Jacob sat down to talk about the blessing Jacob should give for the people of Rich Valley.

"It will not take me long to engrave your blessing on the large white stone once you have crafted it," said Joshua to Jacob.

"No, I am always amazed by how quickly you engrave stone," replied Jacob with a smile. "Perhaps it is because you had such a good teacher when you were young."

"I have no doubt of that, Father," answered Joshua laughing. "You taught me how to engrave beautiful letters into stone."

Just then Faith and Hope came running up to Joshua and jumped on his shoulders.

"Give us a ride, Joshua," yelled Hope.

"Yes, Joshua," said Faith, "take us all the way to the top of the hill."

Joshua balanced the two girls on his back and prepared to give them their ride. He turned to his father as he prepared to start his excursion.

"Be sure to include these two in the blessing, Father," quipped Joshua. "They have both been a blessing to me, even though they do require a lot of my energy."

Jacob laughed as he watched Joshua, Faith, and Hope gallop away on their adventure. He looked at the distant mountains and thought about all the things that had happened since his arrival in Rich Valley.

"I will include them, my son," whispered Jacob. "They have certainly been a blessing to both of us."

A few hours passed before Joseph found Jacob sleeping in the shade of a maple tree, near the large white stone Grace had suggested for the blessing. Joseph gently shook the old man awake and rubbed his shoulders.

"Did you dream well?" asked Joseph softly.

"I'm afraid I was too tired to dream," laughed Jacob. "If I did, I do not remember it well enough to tell you anything."

"I came to tell you I have finished removing the Wizard's evil curse from the tree," said Joseph. "I put some resin and sap where the wood was carved so the great tree can heal. In a few years, no one will be able to tell it was ever carved upon, except for a small scar."

"You have done well, Joseph," said Jacob. "I have completed my thoughts for the blessing Grace proposed to put on the great white rock. Joshua can engrave the letters tomorrow morning in a few hours. That will be in time for the celebration dinner we are to have."

"It will be such a wonderful celebration," declared Joseph. "Faith and Hope have both been practicing some songs they will sing. Grace has cooked enough food to feed a multitude. The people are ready to celebrate all the good things that have happened in Rich Valley."

"The sun is almost down," said Jacob. "We had better get a good night's sleep so we can properly celebrate tomorrow."

Faith, Hope, and Joshua returned from their excursion up the hill as Joseph and Jacob looked at the setting sun.

"Father, we saw five deer and two fox," said Faith excitedly.

"I was the first one to see the fox," exclaimed Hope.

"I am glad you had such a good adventure," said Joseph, "but it is time to go to bed, so you have the energy to sing tomorrow at the celebration."

Joseph, Jacob, and Joshua walked slowly toward Joseph's cabin with Faith and Hope close behind. A slight breeze cooled the air as they walked. Tomorrow would be a celebration. It was a blessing they all looked forward to.

The Final Battle

The smoke from the small campfire curled slowly upward and disappeared into the night sky. Three days of walking had brought the Evil Wizard and his assistant to the Whispering Forest, only a day's walk from Rich Valley. The Wizard sat wearily on a log and watched the smoke vanish in the dark.

"Master, you look so tired," said the evil assistant. "You have not seemed to sleep these last few nights."

"Dark have been my dreams of late," said the Wizard. "I am troubled by my visions of a man I have never met."

"And what is the appearance of this man in your dreams?" inquired the evil helper.

"He appears to be a giant," answered the Wizard, "though I have never seen him in the light of day. He looks at me in my dreams and seems to know me. I cannot tolerate his stare, for he looks at my very soul."

"My lord, there is a witch in this Whispering Forest," said the evil assistant. "It is said she can interpret dreams and see into the future. You could summon her with your powers and perhaps discover who this giant is."

The Wizard stood and stretched his legs before tossing a piece of wood on the fire. He had never before had a dream that troubled him, like his dream about a giant. Maybe the Witch of Whispering Forest could tell him who this giant was.

"Very well," said the Wizard, "I will summon her and see what she can tell me. I may be able to sleep more soundly tonight if I know who the giant stranger is."

The Evil Wizard took some powder from a small pouch in his pocket and threw it onto the fire.

"Veni ad me," cried the Wizard as the powder exploded in the fire.

The evil helper jumped back in fear as a woman with piercing eyes and graying hair suddenly appeared before him.

"It is not often a wizard appears in my woods," said the Witch of Whispering Forest. "What is it you seek from me?"

"I want you to interpret a dream of mine," said the Wizard. "Then I want to know who the man I see in my dreams really is."

The Witch listened to the Wizard's dream before looking into a crystal that hung around her neck on a silver chain.

"You must go back to Ice Mountain," said the Witch firmly. "End your journey now and return to your home. I know you are traveling to Rich Valley, but it is no longer a good place for you."

"Do not tell me what to do, Witch," growled the Wizard. "I only summoned you for information, not advice. Now tell me who the giant in my dreams is."

The Witch looked at the Evil Wizard skeptically. She was not used to people dismissing her advice. She looked once again into her crystal.

"The giant in your dreams is a man who believes in the Creator of all things," said the Witch. "He has the power of knowledge and the power of pure love. There are few people on the earth with both these powers. He is dangerous to you, because he can see inside your spirit. You will meet him if you enter Rich Valley, and he will know who you are."

"I have no fear of this giant," said the Evil Wizard. "I have always had power that caused men to fear me. Why should I not be able to destroy him? If I meet him, he will fear me like all the others."

"If you meet this man, he will see inside your soul," hissed the Witch. "His presence will cause the hate and anger inside you to burn like an unquenchable fire. You will be destroyed from within by your own uncontrollable fury."

The Wizard sat back down on a log gloomily. He stared at the Witch of Whispering Forest. Her reputation was well known on Ice Mountain. Her predictions and interpretations were legendarily accurate, according to those who had dealt with her.

"What payment do you want for your prophecy?" asked the Evil Wizard.

"Your assistant carries some delicious bread with him," answered the Witch. "I will have two loaves of it for my payment."

"It will leave us empty handed when we return from Rich Valley to Ice Mountain," said the Wizard. "Nevertheless, you shall have your bread."

The Witch grabbed the two loaves greedily from the evil assistant and prepared to leave.

"If you go to Rich Valley against my advice, you will have no need for this bread," said the Witch as she disappeared into the night.

"Master, perhaps the Witch is right," cried the evil assistant. "It may be that your spell on Rich Valley did not destroy them as you planned. If they no longer fear you, what will happen when we arrive?"

The Evil Wizard frowned at his evil assistant before uttering a string of curses at the people of Rich Valley.

"We will go to Rich Valley tomorrow. We will see the fear in the eyes of the people who have been left alive after the avalanche," shouted the Wizard. "Then we will tell them of the horror in their future. That is my plan, and it will be carried out."

The evil assistant crept away silently and began preparing his place to sleep. He knew better than to argue with his master. The predictions made by the Witch of Whispering Forest were frightening, but there was little he could do about them. Tomorrow, he and the Evil Wizard would enter Rich Valley. He shivered as he felt a dread he could not explain.

Rachel was the oldest woman in Rich Valley. All the people in the valley knew her as the kindly old woman who shared her garden vegetables with everyone in need. Gentle Rachel was her nickname in the valley. Everyone had at least one story about a time when Rachel had helped them in one way or another. Now Rachel stood below the great pine tree crying. All the people in the valley stood around her to see the great tree, now that Joseph had removed the Evil Wizard's curse from it. Gentle Rachel cried tears of joy. She had seen the fear and sadness the curse had brought the valley. These days, there was a new spirit in the valley, where she had been born. It was a spirit of love and laughter and light.

"I have dreamed of this time for us all," cried Rachel. "The joy has returned to our wonderful valley."

The population of Rich Valley had spent some time at the majestic pine tree. They remembered now how beautiful the tree had been, before the hideous curse had been carved on it. It was a moment for all of them to consider the profound changes that had taken place in Rich Valley.

Presently the entire crowd gathered around the great tree and began sharing the foods they had all brought. No one at the party could remember a time when such feasting was available. Aaron the farmer announced he had devised some trenches to carry the melted snow from the great avalanche to water their crops and trees. It looked like the valley would see a harvest like they had never seen before. Everywhere there was a sense of undeniable optimism.

After the meal, the crowd gathered around Grace, who had promised a surprise blessing for the people of Rich Valley. The crowd of people walked from the great pine tree to the large white stone that marked the boundary of Rich Valley.

"This is the blessing given to us by our friends," announced Grace. "Jacob has written it, and Joshua has engraved it into the great white rock so everyone can see it."

The throng of people crowded around the great white stone and read the engraved letters Joshua had carved earlier that morning:

PEOPLE OF RICH VALLEY, THE TRUTH IS NOW CLEAR
WITH COURAGE AND KINDNESS, WE CAN PUT AWAY FEAR
LET US LIFT UP EACH OTHER AND ALL WE HOLD DEAR
SO OUR JOY IN THIS LIFE WILL ALWAYS BE NEAR
WORKING TOGETHER, WE CAN BUILD A NEW DAY
FAITH, HOPE, AND LOVE WILL SHOW US THE WAY

The people read Jacob's blessing several times before Sarah, the dressmaker, approached Jacob.

"Jacob," said Sarah, "the people have asked me, on their behalf, to thank you for your blessing. I must also tell you; we are all very grateful to you and Joshua for saving us from the great avalanche."

Jacob looked at the crowd of people as he and Joshua stood together.

"My son and I are both proud to help the good people of Rich Valley," said Jacob. "We are grateful to you for the fellowship and friendship you have given to both of us. Now, let us continue our celebration feast with some fine music."

At this, Jacob smiled toward Faith and Hope. Grace acknowledged Jacob's clue and ushered her two performers on to a platform Joseph had built for the celebration feast. Faith and Hope began singing the songs they had practiced for the celebration. At the end of every song, the crowd cheered and clapped, while the two sisters smiled and bowed to the crowd.

For hours, the celebration continued with music from many different people who lived in Rich Valley. Then everyone listened to humorous stories from some of the more amusing people in the valley. Gentle Rachel told the story of the time she had set an apple pie outside to cool, only to discover a family of raccoons had completely devoured it. The people relished the chance to laugh and sing and enjoy each other's company. They had lived too long under the Evil Wizard's curse. Everyone in Rich Valley knew it was time to appreciate the joys of life again.

A few more hours passed in good fellowship before the celebrating began to wind down. It had been a most splendid time for everyone in the valley. There was some good memory for each person to treasure in the day they had just enjoyed. As the people began to prepare to leave, an old man observed two strangers approaching on the road coming into Rich Valley. At first, no one paid much attention to the two figures until suddenly the old man recognized both individuals.

"It is the Evil Wizard," cried the old man, "and the helpful stranger who warned us of the great avalanche."

Every person now focused with keen concern at the two men who slowly approached them. The two men stopped briefly and observed the great pine tree with the Evil Wizard's curse now removed. Then both of them moved purposefully toward the crowd of previously happy people.

The Evil Wizard stared at the residents of Rich Valley with such hatred that it caused many of them to remember the fear they had lived with for so long.

"Who dared to remove my curse of fear from that tree?" the Wizard screamed as he pointed at the great tall pine.

Even as he screamed the question, the Evil Wizard stepped closer and noticed Jacob's blessing engraved in the large white stone:

PEOPLE OF RICH VALLEY, THE TRUTH IS NOW CLEAR
WITH COURAGE AND KINDNESS, WE CAN PUT AWAY FEAR
LET US LIFT UP EACH OTHER AND ALL WE HOLD DEAR
SO OUR JOY IN THIS LIFE WILL ALWAYS BE NEAR
WORKING TOGETHER, WE CAN BUILD A NEW DAY
FAITH, HOPE, AND LOVE WILL SHOW US THE WAY

Now the Wizard burned with an anger and hatred he had never felt before. The Wizard's evil assistant felt the heat from the wizard's body and stepped back. The dark hatred inside the Evil Wizard was burning inside him like a fiery furnace.

"Who wrote these words engraved on this white stone?" yelled the Wizard. "Step forward now, and I will deal out your punishment."

Jacob stepped forward and faced the Evil Wizard. Jacob was a brave man who had faced many dangers in his life. However, the dark power of the Wizard made even him tremble slightly.

"The words you have read, engraved on the white rock, are mine," said Jacob. "I wrote them as a blessing for the people of Rich Valley."

The Evil Wizard stared at Jacob with a malice so powerful that everyone present felt it. It was then that Joseph stepped forward and stood next to Jacob.

"I am a carpenter," announced Joseph, "and it was I who removed your evil curse from the great pine tree."

The Wizard looked at both men now with a bitter hostility raging inside him. It was a look so powerfully vicious that both Joseph and Jacob shuddered.

"You have dared to defy my curse," growled the Wizard. "Now your destruction will be swift and unmerciful. When I have finished with you, you will both wish you had never been born."

Suddenly a giant shadow fell upon the Evil Wizard. The Wizard looked up to see the largest man he had ever seen in his life. Joshua stood in such a way that he blocked the Evil Wizard from moving toward Jacob and Joseph.

"Out of my way, giant," said the Wizard. "I will destroy these two fools that have dared to work against my curse of fear. Then I will deal with you."

"You will not harm my father or my friend," said Joshua. "Your power comes from the fear you create inside the minds of your victims. I do not fear your power, Evil Wizard, for I know who you are. Your days of terror against the innocent are over."

The Evil Wizard looked at Joshua carefully for a moment. Then he remembered the warning from the Witch of Whispering Forest. "The giant you will meet has the power of knowledge and pure love. He will see inside your soul, for he knows who you are." The Wizard suddenly realized he was looking at the giant in his dreams. For the first time in his life, the Evil Wizard felt fear. The fear that had caused the destruction of all his victims now took hold of him.

"I will destroy your father and this meddling carpenter," cried the Wizard. "Then I will destroy you so that none of you are left to oppose my will."

"You will not destroy them, and you will not destroy me," said Joshua calmly. "The hour of your destruction has come. It is justice for all the pure of heart you have shattered."

The Evil Wizard burned inside with an anger and hate, stronger than he had ever felt. The fire inside his soul was something he had always been able to control, but now he felt fear. The fear took away his ability to control the unquenchable fire that burned inside him.

"Nisi morti obnoxia sum," cried the Wizard. Suddenly black smoke began coming out of the Wizard's body. His Evil assistant stepped back, as he felt the heat proceeding from the Evil Wizard's body. The Wizard looked helplessly around him but knew there was no one to save him.

"Nisi morti obnoxia sum," cried the Wizard again, in a voice of despair.

All at once, the Evil Wizard's body burst into flames. The flames shot up into the air like torches set ablaze. The flames grew hotter and brighter as the Wizard's flesh was consumed. The people of Rich Valley looked on in horror as the Wizard burned. The flames of the fire danced in the air like flaming orange creatures. For a few moments, the fire intensified, and then the Evil Wizard's body disappeared inside the bright flames. From the fire, the people heard the Wizard's voice one last time.

"Ego defeci odio mea," screamed the Evil Wizard, and then there was silence.

The mighty fire now ended as quickly as it had begun. As the smoke began to clear, the people stepped forward to see what had become of the Evil Wizard. A pile of black ashes was all that remained of the once powerful sorcerer.

Joseph stooped and picked up a handful of the wizard's ashes.

"What did he mean, Jacob?" asked Joseph. "When he said, 'Nisi morti obnoxia sum?'"

"They are the words of an ancient language," said Jacob. "They mean simply, 'I am doomed.'"

"And what of the other thing he cried in the fire?" asked Joshua. "What was he saying with his last breath?"

"Ego defeci odio mea," said Jacob. "It means, 'I am consumed by my hate.'"

The wizard's evil assistant kneeled down and picked up some ashes that had been his former master.

"It is as though he never existed, save for the evil he did," said the evil assistant. "What will become of me now?"

With a sudden look of terror, the evil assistant started running toward Ice Mountain, never to be seen again.

The people of Rich Valley stood in stunned silence for a long time after the Evil Wizard's death. No one seemed quite sure what they should do. A joyful celebration had been ended with a shocking display of death. The sounds of a joyful gathering had turned suddenly into a dazed silence.

"It is so hard to understand all the things we have been through," said Rachel to Jacob. "What should we do now, considering all the evil we have witnessed and dealt with in our valley?"

Jacob looked toward the west as the sun began to set on Rich Valley. The people slowly gathered around him as he began to speak.

"A few moments ago, I was afraid as I faced the Evil Wizard," said Jacob. "I felt the power of his vicious hate. There was a spirit of darkness and wickedness around him, but I had hope. I believe in the Spirit that created all things. His spirit is a spirit of love and mercy. In my heart, I asked the Spirit of Creation to help me battle the dark spirit that ruled the Evil Wizard. In my life, I have often asked the Spirit of Creation to help me choose the path I should follow. I can never follow it perfectly, but I still pray for His constant guidance."

"Can you help us know the Spirit of all creation, Jacob?" asked Aaron. "Is there a way for us to also find the right path to follow?"

Jacob motioned for Faith and Hope to come and sit next to him. As they sat, Jacob pointed to the little girls he had come to know and love.

"You see these two young girls sitting down in front of you. You know them well, because they sing songs and help their mother heal the sick in this valley. Now, I will tell something else about these two," said Jacob.

He paused as he smiled and looked at Faith and Hope.

"Even though these two are young, they already trust in the love of the Creator who made this world. They have felt His love and power in their lives. There is nothing to stop anyone from calling out to the Spirit of all creation. I believe He wants you to know Him and seek Him. Even a child can find the Creator, if it is in their heart to do so," said Jacob.

"Pray for us then, Jacob," said Gentle Rachel. "Pray that we find the love of the Great Creator and follow the path He shows us."

Jacob beckoned Joshua, Joseph, and Grace to join him as he stood with Faith and Hope. They all joined hands and then faced the people of Rich Valley.

"My son, and my friends, will all pray for the people of this valley. We will ask that all of you who desire to find the love of the Creator will find it. After that, we will hope and pray that He will strengthen you to find the path of truth and love," finished Jacob.

With that, Joseph, Grace, Faith, Hope, and Joshua began praying with Jacob for the people of Rich Valley. They prayed that the people in Rich Valley would find the love of the

Creator in their lives and that they would follow a path that would lead them to truth and joy. The people listened quietly to the prayer and then began to leave and go to their homes. For the people of Rich Valley, there seemed to be a new sense of purpose in their existence. The events of the day had been traumatic, yet as they traveled home, they felt a sense of peace. Then, as the sun began to set on the long, eventful day, Jacob, Joshua, Joseph, Grace, Faith, and Hope joined for one last moment of thanksgiving. They thanked the Creator for all the blessings they had seen in their lives and for finding such valuable friends in each other. And as the sun disappeared on the distant horizon, they praised the Spirit of Creation for the strength to battle all the evils they had faced and for the victory He had given them in the hour of their deliverance.

Epilogue

Some day you may be traveling when you come upon a place called Rich Valley. It is a beautiful place, with people that are full of kindness and generosity toward others. They will show you the gorgeous meadows in their valley. You will see lush green pastures, full of brightly colored flowers, that remind your soul of the splendor of nature. After you walk through the pastures, you will enter a lovely forest, full of wonderful trees offering their shade for your comfort. As you sit beneath the trees, the wind will rustle through their leaves, and it will sound like children playing. The people of Rich Valley will tell you it is two little girls, named Faith and Hope, laughing and singing as they gather berries for their mother, Grace. If you walk a little further, you will come upon a magnificent pine tree. It is the tallest of all the trees, and it stands like a guardian of the precious things in the valley it watches over. There is a small scar on the magnificent tree. It is where a carpenter named Joseph removed an evil curse of fear, carved into its heart long ago. Not far from the extraordinary tree, you will see a great white stone with a blessing from a wise man named Jacob given for the people of Rich Valley:

People of Rich Valley, the truth is now clear
With courage and kindness, we can put away fear
Let us lift up each other and all we hold dear
So our joy in this life will always be near
Working together, we can build a new day
Faith, hope, and love will show us the way

The citizens of Rich Valley will tell you the blessing was engraved into the stone by a giant man named Joshua. They speak in awe of this man of great stature and of pure love. It was he;

they will tell you, more than any other, who saved the valley from the dark curse of evil that once held the valley in its deadly grip. As your day in Rich Valley continues to unfold, you will marvel at all the wonders the valley holds. You will see deep rivers of crystal-clear water, with colorful fish swimming in the frigid waters. You will see every kind of animal you can imagine, enjoying the bounty of life the valley offers. Finally, at the end of your day, when you have finished experiencing all the splendors of Rich Valley, you will prepare to leave. It is then that the people will tell you, to look into the night sky. In the darkness, you will see a million dazzling stars shining in the blackened heavens. If you look closely, the valley residents will tell you, you will see a man in a shining suit looking down at the valley he once visited. And if you listen prayerfully for just a moment, the shiny man will whisper in your ear what he once told a giant long ago, "Remember, dear friend, in the moment when all hope seems lost, somewhere a light is shining."

The End

About the Author

John Callison is a retired schoolteacher from the state of Texas who worked with special needs children for nearly forty years. His experiences caused him to write a book that reflected the struggles he witnessed in the lives of many of his students to find acceptance, hope, love, and faith in their individual lives. His work uses various characters and situations that hopefully portray the quest most people experience as they try to find the love, faith, and hope most of us desire.

CPSIA information can be obtained
at www.ICGtesting.com
Printed in the USA
LVHW020831200520
655963LV00003BA/23